For Felicity J.M.

This edition is
published and distributed
exclusively by
DISCOVERY TOYS
Martinez, CA

First published
in 1988 by
Walker Books, Ltd.
London

Printed in Hong Kong

ISBN 0-939979-23-3

Presents
from
Grandma

Written by
Jan Mark

Illustrated by
Graham Percy

DISCOVERY TOYS

Grandma came to stay.

She came on the train with a bag full of clothes, a bag full of presents and a bag full of knitting.

Mick knew which bag had the knitting in it. He could see the needles sticking out.

Grandma kissed Mom and she kissed Kate, but
she shook hands with Mick. "I've got presents for
you," said Grandma. Mick knew what the presents
would be: knitting.

Dad was at home with the baby.

He had made some tea and while they drank it Grandma unpacked the presents: a scarf for Dad, a shawl for Mom and a blanket for the baby with a kitten on it. Kate had a sweater to wear with her kilt. The sweater was yellow with teddy bears on it.

Mick had a sweater too. It was brown.

Mom said thank you and put on her shawl while Dad put on his scarf and said thank you. Kate said thank you and put on her sweater and the baby blew bubbles under her blanket.

Mick put on his sweater. "Thank you, Grandma," said Mick.

"You look like a real boy in that," said Grandma.

Mick knew he was a real boy. Grandma didn't have to tell him, but he wanted teddy bears too.

Grandma stayed for two weeks and knitted.

Wherever they went, Grandma was knitting.

She could even watch television and knit.

At the end of her visit they had more presents.
There was a bonnet for the baby with daisies
on it. Kate had a beret and mittens that matched.
There were birds on both.

Mick had a hat and gloves. They were navy blue.
"Boys like plain things," said Grandma.

"I like birds," said Mick.

"Big boys don't want birds," said Grandma.

"Say thank you," said Mom. Grandma had knitted her a frilly top.

Dad had a sweater. It was plain, like Mick's.

Grandma went home on the train. Mom stayed at home with the baby, but Dad and Mick and Kate went to see Grandma off at the station. When the train pulled out, Grandma was already knitting again – something dark and purple and plain.

"I bet that's for me," said Mick.

Mick was right.

After a while a parcel came and inside was a plain purple sweater. "For Mick to wear at school in September," said Grandma's note. There was also a pullover for Kate with penguins on it, and a pink coat for the baby, with pom-poms all over.

Mick wrote to Grandma. "Thank you," he wrote.
He did not mention pom-poms or penguins. He knew
what Grandma would say: "Boys like *plain* things."

September came but Mick did not go back to school. He caught mumps instead and stayed at home with a fat neck. When Mick began to feel better, Kate and the baby caught mumps as well.

"Would you like to go and stay with Grandma while everyone else is ill?" asked Mom. So Mick got into the car and Dad drove him to Grandma's house.

Mick was afraid that he would have to sit and watch Grandma knit for a week, but Grandma put her needles away and rolled up the yarn and said, "What shall we do? We could go to the park, or the river, or the zoo, or we could stay here and paint the fence."

Mick wanted to paint the fence.

They painted the fence all day. After dinner
Grandma got out her needles and some brown yarn.

"I'll knit you a sweater while you're here," said
Grandma, and Mick thought, Oh dear. Something
plain.

He said, "That bit at the bottom of sweaters is like
a fence."

"You mean the ribbing?" asked Grandma.
"I suppose it is."

"I bet you can't make the ribbing like a real fence," said Mick.

"I can try," Grandma said. She forgot about being plain and fetched some white yarn too. She knitted a fence.

"And a tree," Mick said, "behind the fence."

So Grandma fetched green yarn and red, and knitted a tree full of apples before bedtime.

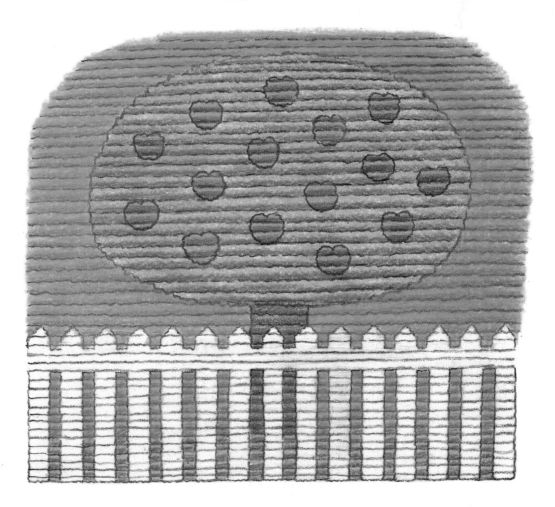

Next day they went to the river and watched the boats. Then they came home and after dinner Grandma took out her needles.

"I'll do a sleeve tonight," said Grandma.

"I bet you can't knit boats," said Mick.

"I bet I can," Grandma said. "Blue yarn and white yarn, please." Mick fetched the yarn and by bedtime Grandma had knitted the river. A canoe and two boats were sailing up the sleeve.

They spent the next day in the park. Mick watched a boy flying a kite and Grandma brought out her knitting.

"There's room on that sleeve for a boy and a kite," said Mick, and before they went home Grandma had knitted the boy flying his kite, all the way up the sleeve.

"Shall we go to the zoo?" Grandma asked the next day. So they went to the zoo and Grandma didn't knit a thing because there was so much to see.

When they got home, Grandma took out her
knitting.

"I bet you can't knit a gorilla," said Mick.

"I can knit anything," said Grandma, "but a gorilla
will take a long time. I can't get it done tonight."

The next day Grandma knitted a gorilla on the back of Mick's sweater and Mick played with the boy next door. He had a tortoise. When Mick came in for dinner he said to Grandma, "Is there room for a tortoise too?"

"It will have to go up in the sky," said Grandma.
"That's all right," said Mick. "I'd like a flying
tortoise."

When Mick went home he wore his sweater.
Kate's neck was thin again and she met him on the
doorstep.

"This is my vacation," said Mick, and he turned
all round so that she could see.

"I want one like that," said Kate.

"It won't always fit me," said Mick. "When I
grow out of my vacation, you can wear it."

"Well done, son," said Mick's dad.
"Can you get her to knit one
like that for me?"